To Joshua, who was born finding words!
Love from Mom
—K.E.H.

To Twin B, my other half.
Love from Twin A
—D.K.H.

ISBN 0-439-68064-6

Text copyright © 2003 by Kathryn Heling and Deborah Hembrook.
Illustrations copyright © 2003 by Patrick Joseph. All rights reserved.
Published by Scholastic Inc., 557 Broadway, New York, NY 10012, by arrangement
with Random House Children's Books, a division of Random House, Inc.
SCHOLASTIC and associated logos are trademarks and/or registered
trademarks of Scholastic Inc.

12 11 10 9 8 7 6 5 4 3 2   4 5 6 7 8 9/0

Printed in the U.S.A.   23

First Scholastic printing, September 2004

MOUSE'S Hide-and-Seek Words

A Phonics Reader

by Kathryn Heling
& Deborah Hembrook
illustrated by Patrick Joseph

SCHOLASTIC INC.

New York   Toronto   London   Auckland   Sydney
Mexico City   New Delhi   Hong Kong   Buenos Aires

Words are here,
words are there.
Little words hide
everywhere!

Look in big words.

Take a peek.

Find a small word—

hide-and-seek!

Mouse rides a train.

train

It starts to rain.

rain

Mouse gets a plate.

plate

He is too late.

late

Mouse pulls the string.
string

Now the bells ring.

ring

Mouse breaks his stool.

stool

He works with a tool.

tool

Mouse wants to stop.

stop

But he hikes to the top.

top

Mouse hears a shout.

shout

Crow yells,
"Look out!"

out

Mouse waters his plants . . .

plants

with help from ants.

ants

Mouse buys a treat.
treat

Now he can eat.

eat

Look at Mouse throw!

throw

He wins three in a row!

row

Mouse starts to trip.

trip

Oops! His pants rip!

rip

The sun is too bright.

bright

Now it is just right.

right

Mouse likes to spend.

spend

But this is the end.

end

Mouse's hide-and-seek
is done.

Playing word games
is such fun!

Keep on looking here and there—
words are hiding everywhere!